A Ferret in a Garret

An ode to Jackson Pollock

Written by Peter Hoffman
Illustrated by Cindy Olson

A FERRET IN A GARRET

An ode to Jackson Pollock

Peter Hoffman

Written by Peter Hoffman
Illustrated by Cindy Olson

Published by artpacks
Rochester, Minnesota 507/273/2529

Trajan Pro, Cooper Black, and Quadraat Sans are the fonts used in this book.
The illustrations are rendered in watercolor and colored pencil.

Library of Congress Cataloging-in-Publication Data

Hoffman, Peter, 1987-
  A ferret in a garret / by Peter Hoffman ; [illustrations by Cindy Olson]. – 1st ed.
      p. cm.
  "This book is based on a poem that Peter Hoffman wrote when he was in fifth grade. Illustrator, Cindy Olson, was Peter's elementary school art teacher."
  Summary: A ferret's late-night visit to Jackson Pollock's Long Island, New York, art studio inspires the budding artist to develop a new style of painting.
  ISBN 978-0-9790247-6-4 (hardcover : alk. paper)
  1. Pollock, Jackson, 1912-1956 – Juvenile fiction. 2. Children's writings. [1. Stories in rhyme. 2. Pollock, Jackson, 1912-1956 – Fiction. 3. Ferret – Fiction.
  4. Painting – Technique – Fiction. 5. Children's writings.] I. Olson, Cindy, 1968- ill. II. Title.

  PZ8.3.H6755Fer 2008
  [E]–dc22
            2008002368

This book is dedicated to Alister, my wonderful sleeping dog.

P.H.

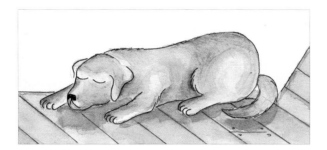

For Eric, Hannah, Nick, and Margaret.

C.O.

A young artist is struggling, then suddenly gets mad.
His paintings are so boring, not like the visions he has had!

Bold, jazzy visions pulse in his head,

But he can't seem to paint them, so he stomps off to bed.

In the middle of the night as the artist sleeps,
Outside in the dark, something creeps.

As the moonlight slowly comes down from the sky,
It catches something – a ferret's eye!

The ferret quietly creeps from his hole,
Straight to the artist's garret he strolls.

**Inside the light is soft and faint.
He gets an idea! He sees the paint!**

He jumps up on the table and knocks down the red,
It falls a few feet from a sleeping dog's head.

The paint makes a bold, squiggly design.
Some may think it looks awful, to the ferret it looks fine!

He knocks down some orange, some green, and some yellow,

And starts to feel a lot like this cool artist fellow.

Then a clock strikes loudly, it's close to dawn.

The dog starts stirring – "Time to be gone!"

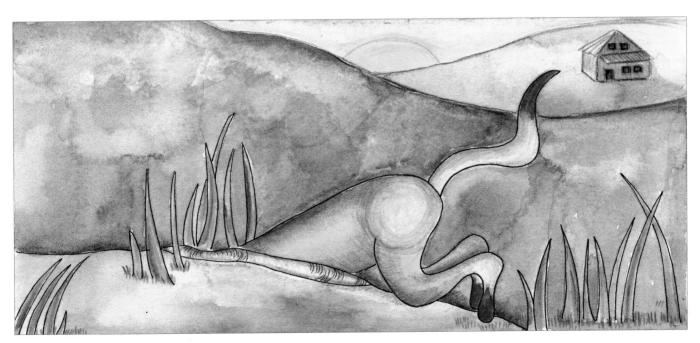

**The ferret runs from the garret back into his hole,
As quiet as a rabbit, a mouse, or a mole.**

He hangs up his hat and slinks off to bed,

As visions of a new art dance in his head.

Then the young artist wakes up and goes back to his garret

and sees the paint on the floor left by the ferret.

He likes the movement!

He likes the action!

All of this really influenced Jackson.

Soon all of Pollock's paintings came from the heart.

He started to drip paint and do Abstract Art.

His fame spread like fire from "highland" to highland.

Soon there was no one more famous on all of Long Island.

Pollock became an art icon from his start in the garret.
But now we all know that at least some of the credit,

Should go to a cunning, clever young ferret.

Back Story: How Peter's Jackson Pollock Ferret Was Born

By Julie Anne Hoffman

"A Ferret In A Garret" first appeared in print nine years ago on page fifty-five of the 1999 edition of *Falcon Tales*, the yearly collection of prose and poetry written by the students of Folwell Elementary School where Peter was a fifth grader. Peter knew he would be heading off to middle school the next year, and he was excited to make his last effort for the publication extra special.

"Mom!" I remember him saying, coming into the kitchen and interrupting me making dinner. "I know what I'm going to write about for *Falcon Tales* – ferrets!"

I stopped stirring the spaghetti sauce and slipped into what I have to admit was less than my best June Cleaver moment.

"Ferrets! Come on, Peter." I remember replying testily. Peter had this silly thing about ferrets. He would always insist on stopping at Brink's Pet Store where a visit to the ferret cage always ended up with him begging me to buy one. He had even started a comic strip – "As Good As It Gets" – with a ferret as its main character. This was getting to be a little too much, I remember thinking, and I decided a little "subtle" parental redirection was needed.

"Why is it always ferrets?" I asked, my voice rising. "Peter, I just spent six weeks teaching art to your class. I dragged all that stuff back from the Jackson Pollock show (in New York City) – you even just wrote a paper on Pollock – and all you can think of are ferrets! And you can forget about getting a ferret with Alister (our yellow Labrador); he'd rip it apart. So why don't you write about something else?"

Peter quietly waited for me to finish, then said: "There's just one problem."

"What's that?" I answered.

"I can't think of anything that rhymes with ferret," he said.

Giving up, I answered: "Garret. Garret rhymes with ferret."

"That's great!" Peter said. "But what's a garret?"

"It's where an artist works," I answered, sprinkling a little more basil into the sauce.

Peter smiled, disappeared into the toy room, and, about an hour later, proudly handed me a lined, yellow piece of paper with the words, " 'A Ferret In A Garret' by Peter Hoffman," written at the top, and this book's poem written below.

Filled with delightfully rhymed stanzas, the poem tied Peter's love for ferrets to Jackson Pollock's art, in a whimsical tale that credited a mischievous mammal as the inspiration for Pollock's breakthrough "drip" paintings that set the modern art world atwitter in the 1950s.

"Peter, this would make a terrific kid's book," I said. "And I know the perfect person to illustrate it – Cindy (Olson, his Folwell art teacher)."

Nine years later, this is exactly what happened, proving that, sometimes, wonderful things can occur when you don't – well, sort of don't – listen to your mother!